AUTHOR'S INTRODUCTION

Greetings, I am W.S. Ishida, the author of *The Lost Chapters,* a collection of vignettes set in the heart of the British countryside during the 1950s. There are seven in total, all told in a colloquial style from the perspective of the narrator, Rosemary Page, as she looks back on some of her formative experiences in growing up. These short stories chart her life at various ages, detailing the trials and tribulations as she navigates childhood and prepares for adulthood.

Actually... calling them short stories may be a little bit of a fib - please let me explain. These shorts were originally chapters in my debut novel, *Goodbye to Ribbons,* but despite much pleading, begging, and beseeching from me, I eventually obeyed my editor's demands and duly removed these much-loved chapters from the final manuscript.

Q. If I loved them so much, why did they need to be removed?

Ah, good question. Well, the short answer is for the sake of brevity as the novel was becoming monstrously long. Going into further detail, it was also deemed necessary for the balance of the plot relating to the protagonist's ageing.

Although originally written as chapters, they still hold their own as individual pieces - or perhaps best described as slice-of-life vignettes, or even what some people may call short stories! Anyway, I am very pleased these orphaned chapters have now been given a home they can call their own.

Please enjoy...

A Confession

One final thing, if I may - I'm all for honesty and being up front, so I freely admit that as well as wanting my hard work to find grateful eyes, these previously orphaned chapters are also being put to work - namely in the marketing department for my debut novel. My hope is that you enjoy them and the style of my writing enough to consider reading the full-length novel, ***Goodbye to Ribbons.*** Further information on the full novel can be found at the end of this book, including an extra bonus sneak peak of the opening three chapters.

Note on the Bonus Content: Author's Insight

After each short story, I have included two sections of insight and analysis. The first section, after each vignette, considers the story as an individual piece of writing. Whereas the second also considers the story's relationship to the full novel they were originally taken from.

Of course, please feel free to skip these and get straight to the next story if you so wish.

W.S. Ishida

CONTENTS

GOODBYE TO RIBBONS

W.S. Ishida

wsishida.com

ISBN: 978-1-8381953-4-2

Paperback Edition

THE LOST CHAPTERS

7 SHORT STORIES FROM THE BRITISH COUNTRYSIDE

W.S. ISHIDA

FAUX CROW
PUBLISHING

1

OL' BESSIE THE FLYING HORSE

(1955 ~ AGED 10)

Even when sick and confined to our beds, trouble always seemed to have the knack of sniffing us out. When my two older brothers and me came down with the mumps, we all had to sleep in the one bed so that the young'uns, Perry and Puddin, didn't get sick too.

Anyway, with us older ones being cooped up like hens in a hut, it wasn't long before we started getting cabin fever and making amusements for ourselves. The boys mostly played marbles but that didn't interest me. My favourite game was to ride the antique clotheshorse my parents had got as a wedding present.

I'd always be sure to fold up any clothes and put them safely aside before I saddled her up. I called her Bessie and would brush her down after a hack, feed her imaginary sugar-cubes (always remembering to keep my palm nice and flat), then give her a reassuring pat and talk all quiet to her like you should. It'd been a dream of mine, for as long as I could remember, to have a real horse. And I always knew inside of me that one day I would make that come true.

I didn't pay no mind to the boys when they teased me for pretending away with Bessie; we'd just ignore them, knowing that really they were jealous.

On day three of our confinement, Billy finally got bored of playing marbles and asked if he could ride Bessie. I felt like denying him, but I couldn't—I was too excited. It was usually always me having to go along with other people's games, so I wanted nothing more than to share my world for once.

First, I let him feed her a sugar-cube. "No, keep your palm nice and flat—if you want to keep your fingers that is," I told him. "Ok, good. Now, gently stroke her nose." This was so she would feel comfortable with him before he got on.

He was a bit unsure at first and kept checking back at Karl, but Karl was pretending to be busy with his marbles.

"We'll just take her for a little tramp down toward the meadow and see how you get on from there," I said as I tightened the girth. "Since it's your first time an' all."

"We gonna do some jumps though, aren't we?" Billy said, much louder than was necessary.

"We'll see, we'll see."

I took it nice and gentle at the beginning and

kept talking to Bessie, letting her know it was alright. She seemed pretty happy with the two of us riding her, so when we reached the fens I decided to see how brave Billy really was, and took her up to a canter. He seemed to be enjoying it and Bessie seemed to be holding up okay, so I dug the stirrups into her sides once again and set her into a gallop. She gave a whinnying neigh before lengthening her stride and stretching her head further forwards. The wind streamed my long, dark hair back into Billy's face as he gripped tightly to my nightdress. Faster and faster we went, the hawthorn hedges soon becoming a blur. We flew across the meadows to the pounding rhythm of hooves. Bessie's brisk snorts of breath pluming into the frigid morning air, like an unstoppable steam train thundering through the countryside. I turned back to check on Billy. His eyes were watering but he managed a smile.

"You wanna jump then?" I shouted.

He nodded eagerly.

"Better hold on tight!" I spurred her on with a couple more kicks. Then pulling on the left rein, I lined her up toward a low grassy rise just before a dyke.

"You have to move up with her when she jumps," I shouted back.

"You what?"

"You have to-" but it was too late, we were upon it.

Bessie gathered her stride before leaping forward

and clearing the dyke with ease. Billy bumped and bounced but thankfully didn't come a cropper.

"Move *up* when she jumps, and down again when she lands," I told him.

"Right . . . "

If he didn't quite get it the first time, by about the third he'd figured it out and was giving great whoops of delight each time Bessie took to the air.

"Right, gel," I said leaning forward and whispering in her ear, "let's really give him a show, shall we."

We'd travelled a fair distance, way past the mill, past the pillbox, and all the way down past the cow tower. Bessie and I had been out this way a few times before, so we'd already eyed-up a hedge that I'd fancied having a go at. It was pretty high, but it was the thickness that made it a real challenge. Like a fat, bristling, green monster it wormed its way across the countryside. I knew it was doable and I knew it would do the job of scaring the pants off Billy too.

The meadow leading to it was on a downward slope, so our speed naturally picked up. "Remember what I told yuh, and you better hold on!" I shouted to Billy, as I gripped tighter with my knees.

"What, we gonna . . . ? That!"

I pushed his hand down. "I said - *hold on*."

"But we'll never . . . "

As the green giant grew larger, we were left with only two choices: go through it, or go over it.

I could feel every muscle in Bessie winding up as

she gathered her stride, and then with a rallying neigh we launched, and over it we flew, and I mean *flew*. It was as if we were riding a winged unicorn, gravity forgotten, soaring through the air, the world so far beneath us everything went quiet. All I could feel was the wind on my face and tussling through my hair, until a rising tingle inside told me we'd started coming back down to Earth. As if in slow motion we began to fall, the green of the grass far below coming back into focus.

I ent really sure why, maybe it was because Bessie wasn't as young as I supposed, or that we'd got caught up in the excitement and had jumped too high and too fast, or maybe it was just the extra weight—who knows. But we landed with a jarring thud. Then I felt Bessie stumble as her front legs buckled, followed by a sickly—*snap*! And down we went. Tumbling into a heap on the old threadbare rug.

As soon as we'd untangled ourselves, I sprung up to check on Bessie. Her front leg was broke clean in two, and a huge split ran down her side. I knew straight off—it was the glue factory for her and no mistake. But, I also knew there was no time to grieve.

The three of us looked to each other.

Everything was deathly calm.

Me and Billy both held our breath.

Then finally—the distant *BOOM, BOOM, BOOM* of feet pounding up the wooden stairs.

Dad was already hollering before he even knew what we'd done. I turned to Billy, the fear in his eyes a mirror of my own, whilst Karl looked on with a smug, *I told you so,* grin.

There was a spilt second silence between the footsteps stopping and Dad bursting through the door in his socks and underwear.

"What in hell is going on!" he thundered.

He took in the scene—but not to work out *what* had happened, but to work out *who* he should grab first.

Seeing a chance I reacted, and the next thing I knew I'd bolted for the gap between him and the door. I don't know what happened behind me but it seems Billy, fearing he was about to cop my beating, followed quickly on my heels. However, making a run for it marked me out as the prime suspect, so Dad turned to give chase.

I reached the top of the stairs and was inches from freedom when they both came pouring out onto the landing. I glanced over my shoulder to see Dad towering up behind me. His leg drew back, then shot forwards as he aimed a kick at my backside. All I could do was flatten myself against the banister and watch his grey-socked foot go flying past my face. At the same time Billy tried to stop but slipped on the rug and took out Dad's standing leg. With both legs now in the air he landed on his bum and bounced all the way down those steep wooden stairs.

We wasted little time in bolting back into the bedroom and grabbing poor Bessie and jamming her tight up against the handle. And there we sat for quite some time, bracing the door, wondering if we'd ever get out of there alive.

Thankfully his anger would often pass as quickly as it came on, and so we knew there was always a chance of dodging the belt if we could take shelter until the storm blew itself out.

To be honest, it was rare that we got a beating that we thought we didn't have coming. Mostly we considered ourselves just plain unlucky, because no matter how hard we tried, we always seemed to find a way of getting wrong. So eventually, we just had to accept that trouble was always going to be one of our closest play mates.

AUTHOR'S INSIGHT: OL' BESSIE THE FLYING HORSE

This piece is predominantly about the potential and importance of childhood imagination. An active imagination can provide so many things - such as escapism, even when quarantined in a small bedroom. It can also allow children to practice aspects of life and gain experience by playing out certain roles that may otherwise not be within their current sphere of experience. In this case, Rosie, the youngest of the three children who are cooped up in the room, and the only female, get's a chance to be the leader, to be the one in charge, to take on the responsibility of leading the adventure. She tells us that usually she is the one having to tag along and join in with her brothers' make-believe worlds, so she plainly revels in the newfound power dynamic as she finally gets an opportunity to give advice and warnings to her older brother.

A common theme you may notice throughout this

collection is that of children's natural ability to get in to trouble without trying to or even realising it, until it's too late. Which arguably is an essential component of growing up, of learning, and gaining invaluable experience in life. However, in this story, it's their over exuberance, their experimentation in pushing the boundaries of play, and then ultimately losing themselves so completely in their fantasy world, that proves to be their undoing.

This short also touches on the pressures of the expected gender roles that children often experience and how this may affect their interactions with one another. They can often feel funnelled into certain expectations. Billy is clearly a very willing participant in what may be deemed as a *girls'* game by society, but still feels the need to play this down in front of his older brother, Karl. Another intention in this piece is to suggest that Karl also wishes he could join in, and is casting a jealous eye that is disguised as contempt. That if he had felt comfortable enough to be honest too, they could've all enjoyed playing together.

In order to make this piece more visceral, the description of the imaginary world quickly merges into reality. Rosie also begins to narrate it as if she and her brother are simultaneously experiencing the same things in same moment as they unfold, such as when she aims the horse towards the large hedge. Billy immediately understands her intention without the need for it to be vocalised. They are so immersed in the world that they both see the same pictures.

The fact Billy feels the need to question her decision to jump the big hedge, further cements the fact that this is now real, with real consequences. Until finally the journey into their imagination comes crashing back to earth.

In relation to the full novel:

This was perhaps the hardest of all chapters to cut from the final novel, *Goodbye to Ribbons*. I feel this short worked hard at successfully setting-up and cementing many of Rosie's characteristics, such as her tendency for escapist flights of fantasy. This trait still remains in the novel, but this early example here is so strong and visceral that it briefly absorbs and takes over reality as she recounts the tale. Another key function of it within the novel was to set-up her long-held love for and desire to one day own a horse.

Another important role I felt this chapter performed was in showing her early experiences of navigating relationships in a predominantly man's world. With so many brothers, she has plenty of practice, that later stands her in good stead to be somewhat of a gender-role-defying pioneer in her working life. It also foreshadows a natural ability to adapt to a situation and manage people who would normally be expected to hold power over her. Later in the novel, her tendency to hide these innate personality traits away and to instead default to or resort to servitude, is one of the fundamental problems she must overcome. This chapter helped to show she has that latent potential, and that perhaps she just needs to carve out the correct environment to allow it to flourish.

This chapter also shows the fear their father held over them as children, and hints at the anger he harbours. It also introduced the symbolism of storms and wind, often used in a metaphorical sense when she talks about her parents. And finally, whilst being careful not to provide any spoilers, it begins to show her father is also prone to an almost fatalist acceptance of defeat and a lack of will to truly put up a fight - seen in this chapter, when he fails in his attempt to exact punishment and is presumably left somewhat humiliated in the process.

Hmm, tell me again, why did I allow this chapter to be removed? Do you think my editor will let me squeeze it back in?

{No. Love, Ed.]

2

DENY, DENY, DENY!

(1956 ~ AGED 11)

We weren't wrong'uns and certainly never set out looking for it, but like most children, trouble always seemed to have a knack of finding us. Often, we'd just be playing and causing no one no harm, when the next thing you know fellas are rushing past your kitchen window with buckets of water as they race to put out the hay-barn you'd set on fire.

This time I had a new partner in crime. With my older brother Billy having out-grown me, his boots were filled by my younger brother Perry. He was almost two years my junior and therefore not yet allowed out of the garden by himself. I was still only 11, but finding myself as the eldest of the duo meant I got my first real taste of being the boss.

Now, across the road from our house and down the loke was a small pond. It wasn't quite deep enough to swim in, but it was big enough to keep a couple of kids interested for an hour or so. One end was crowded out by an ancient weeping willow that dangled its tassely hair into the pond's murky green water, teasing soft swirling patterns in the floating algae. At the other end, a half-sunk boat could be made good as a jetty, and it was from there, late one afternoon, that we were tiddlin for minnows. We had a fair few swimming around in our glass jar before Perry got bored. Instead, he sat on the bank and began fishing in his pockets until he came out with a box of matches.

"Look what I got, Rosie," he said, holding them up proudly.

"Well then, best we light a fire. That's what you do when you go fishing," I told him with authority.

"Yeah?"

"Yeah. Just a little one mind," I said, not forgetting my responsibilities of course.

So we gathered some loose hay from the nearby barn and soon had ourselves a little fire crackling away.

Being brought up in the countryside, you needed a fair bit of common sense about you, because most of the time you were off on your tod and not always within yelling distance of an adult. So when dinnertime came around, I knew enough that you don't leave no fire going by itself. I tipped a bit of water out from our tiddlin jar onto it – though not too much as I didn't want to leave the minnows without. Then, not wanting to get the belt from Dad for being late, we rushed off home.

After scrubbing-up, we sat at the big wooden table ready to eat, both hungry as a horse after a hard day's work. But, barely had our dinner been dished-up when Mr Craker came pelting down the path, all panicked and hollering for our dad.

"Trevor! Trevor! Quick! Quick! It's the effin hay-barn!" he was screaming, eyes wide and wild, face red.

Well, I'd never felt so queer so quickly in all my short life. I looked over at Perry to see the colour had gone from him too. But I also saw he wasn't looking at me. I turned slowly towards the kitchen window. From across the road and down past the loke, gret ol' barrels of dark grey smoke were rolling up into the sky, endlessly, one after another.

There was no hiding the guilt plastered all over our faces. It would've only taken a glance at either of us to find the culprits in a second, so I thought for sure that at any moment one of my father's big grimy hands was going to grab us by the scruff of our necks and haul us off for a belting. However, such was the panic, that anyone too small to carry a bucket of water was instantly ignored.

Meanwhile, the flames were clawing so high into the sky that the grown-ups were worried it was gonna spread to the nearby houses. With my hunger all but forgotten, I slid down from my chair and slunk off to the bedroom. Whereas the rest of the boys were crowded eagerly around the window, as if they were watching a television show.

Just as I was going into the bedroom, I heard

someone behind me on the stairs. I felt the hairs tiptoe up the back of my neck, but when I turned it was just little Perry.

"What we gonna do, Rosie?" he whispered.

He looked so small and fragile, but I didn't know what to say, so I got angry with him and sent him off to bed too. All I could think to do was hide under my covers and hope sleep would come early, and then come the morning all would be forgotten and everything back to normal.

Well... all was certainly not forgotten.

The next morning arrived, and with it two policemen knocking at the door. You always knew someone was in trouble when *two* police came a-knocking.

We all got questioned, and once Perry let on we'd been down at the pond—the pond that was no more than fifty yards from the hay-barn—I couldn't see any possible way out of a belting and whatever it might be the police would do to us.

No, we hadn't been playing with no matches.

No, we hadn't been smoking cigarettes.

No, we hadn't been near that hay-barn.

No, we hadn't seen no suspicious characters.

All we could do was deny, deny, deny.

No, we wouldn't lie to a policeman.

"Hmph. They're tell'un truths, this time," Dad finally grunted, having felt we'd had enough of a grillin. "All of 'em were eating dinner here when it happened," he told the policemen.

Well, we couldn't quite believe it! Of all the people, it was the executioner himself that had turned out to be our saviour.

Many years later, when we were all grown up, we were having one of them good 'ol reminisces about the old'n times, when Perry let it slip about the hay-barn.

"You mean... that was you? You little buggers!" my father said. "You made me lie to a police officer?"

But by then, we were too old and my father too weak for us to get the belt, so we all had a good chuckle over it.

AUTHOR'S INSIGHT: DENY, DENY, DENY!

Deny, Deny, Deny is about children tasting responsibility for the first time. Like the first story, it's also about childhood experimentation, growing and playing at being adults - after all, from a kid's perspective it doesn't look that difficult, right?

However, Rosie soon learns that life is more complicated that she can yet grasp. Even though she thought she'd done the right thing in remembering to put out the small fire, in her haste to get back in time for dinner (what she perceived as the most important duty to attend to), she doesn't take care of the responsibility that ultimately harbours the biggest consequences. In fact, the two decisions that she regards as the most sensible and prioritises, ultimately prove to be her undoing. Namely:

1. *Ensuring they are not late for dinner (showing her respect - or fear for authority).*

2. *Not using too much of the minnows' water (showing her caring side and capability of forethought).*

Both are admirable and important considerations, unfortunately as it transpires in these circumstances - not *the* most important.

This short also, to an extent, comments on the fallibility of adults - to quote from the actual novel, *"As a child, you think adults are like gods, they never make mistakes."* Yes, Rosie makes mistakes by not ensuring the fire is extinguished, and if she had've been caught she would've fully expected to suffer the consequences exacted by the god-like adults. However, there is a hint here that adults are not as perfect and all-knowing as she may have assumed - or they may like to pretend.

This is evident when the children are ignored in the face of having to deal with the raging inferno. However, as Rosie puts it, *"it would've only taken a glance at either of us to find the culprits"*. Further more, just as the incriminating evidence begins to stack up against them and it seems they will inevitably be caught, the father inadvertently saves them by mistakenly providing them with a false alibi to the police. She begins to see they too make mistakes and oversights.

Finally, this piece comments on how time often smoothes the edges of history. Back when the incident happened, it was very serious. Houses and maybe lives could've been at risk, to the extent that the police became involved. It's suggested that the father would have been raging more than the inferno, had he realised it was Rosie and Little Pea who started the fire. But years later, with enough distance to mellow the mood, it instead becomes a nostalgic, humorous memory, and the much-feared father is able to see the funny side now that they are all adults - now that Rosie and Lil' Pea understand their mistake and the severity of it.

In relation to the full novel:

One of the main purposes this chapter served in the novel was to set-up why Rosie believes she is almost cursed. Everything she is involved with, despite her best efforts to steer them in the opposite direction, seem to take a turn for the worse.

Previously in the novel, she has always had to be content with the role of sidekick in their early adventures. But now she is the oldest of the two-sibling adventure party, she gets her first taste of authority and believes she is up to the task, and therefore takes it seriously. Yet (what becomes a major motif in the novel and she notes herself) somehow *"life always finds a way of sneaking up behind you and biting you on the bum."* Things always seem to backfire and go wrong for her, to such an extent that it culminates in her feeling like she has become no more than a helpless passenger as her life turns into a headlong downward spiral.

This chapter was also important in setting up the ever-present lurking fear of their father and the beltings he would administer for their wrongdoings. And as previously mentioned, it subtly foreshadows her eventual discovery that adults aren't infallible, they aren't the gods they may purport to be.

UNCLE SID BARRET

(TAKEN FROM THE CHAPTER MY MARVELLOUS MOTHER IN THE NOVEL)

[NOTE: I haven't counted this one as one of the seven stories as it is more an extract.]

Everyone thought she was marvellous. You asked anyone and they'd say she was the salt of the earth, a real good un, always ready to help others out. This meant we often had folks staying over at ours. So much so, for a time I thought we actually ran some sort of guesthouse.

The most regular was 'Uncle' Sidney Barrett, who would come down most Fridays on his pony and trap with a Sunday joint of meat tucked under his arm - though I'm pretty sure he didn't ride the whole way like that. Anyway, he always stayed two nights, and then after Mum had cooked up the joint for Sunday dinner and we'd put pay to it with our bellies, he'd head back home to his farm again, ready for work on Monday morning.

Whether or not his wife knew I don't know, but the reason he'd come visiting so regular was because she didn't like him drinking. My mum would let him come stay at ours so he could spend the whole weekend in the pub getting brarmsed without worrying about upsetting *"her indoors,"* as he put it.

On the Saturday's, when he was down our way, Mum was insistent that every single one of us kids had to go to the pub with him. We were never really sure why at the time, but you don't think to ask questions at that age, you just blindly do whatever adults (and especially your parents) tell you. Not that we minded one bit though, as Sid always gave us enough money to go to the pictures and get a bag of crisps each.

"Whhhen yurr finished, you know where'ta find me," he'd say.

But where we found him, depended on exactly how brarmsed he'd got at the pub. If he'd only got a bit squiffy, he'd mostly be found singing in Queen's Square and eating prawns. But . . . if he'd got really tanked-up, we'd usually find him halfway home slumped over a gate or in a hedge, having completely forgotten he was meant to be waiting for us. If he was still able to make a sentence, it was always the same.

"Your mum's a good sort, y'know. Don't let no one tell yuh any different. She looks arter me, dun't she," he'd say, over and over again the whole way home.

AUTHOR'S INSIGHT: UNCLE SID

This very short piece comments on the importance of perspective in any given situation. From the mother's perspective, she is doing an old friend a favour in facilitating his weekends of drunkenness. However, would Uncle Sid's wife see it that way? Especially if the drinking is a problem for him, or a bone of contention in their relationship. So the question is raised - is the marvellous mother really performing a kindness for him or not?

Similar to the previous shorts, this one also asks questions regarding responsibility. The onus would naturally fall upon Sid to act as the responsible adult when taking the children into town, yet he pays them off with cinema tickets and snacks so he can go off and do his drinking undisturbed. And then, it transpires that it is actually the children who bear the brunt of being responsible, as it is left to them to seek him out and make sure *he* gets home safely.

This also brings into question the mother's level of responsibility. Does she know the full details of the arrangement between Sid and the kids? If she does, does she mind? Is she insistent that the kids go with him, through altruistic motives because she is aware that Sid can't always control his drinking, so therefore requires the help to get home? Or is it for more personal reasons such as just wanting to have time to herself without a whole load of kids crazing her and getting under her feet?

Also, it reflects on the times when the countryside children of yesteryear had to be more savvy and accept more responsibility than perhaps their modern counterparts do nowadays. And at the same time, they were also afforded more freedom because the times were perceived to be safer.

In relation to the full novel:

This extract from a chapter was intended to lay some foundations and hints for some of Rosemary's mother's behaviour that is revealed later in the novel. Partly, in showing her desire to be kind and generous towards others, but also to show how she is prepared to bend her morals within her role/quest as the Good Samaritan. It also provides a very subtle hint towards the slightly more devious acts she engages in too - but I've said too much already...

A prominent theme that features in the novel, that of escape and running away from problems rather than facing up to them, is also reinforced by

Uncle Sid as he seeks escape from the strictures of his home life. This piece also serves the purpose of setting the seeds for the tone of a slightly recklessness and care-free attitude that was sometimes prevalent after the war and more especially in the deeper countryside were things weren't so tightly policed. Therefore it doesn't seem so out of kilter when aspects of reckless behaviour happen later in the novel to a much greater degree.

3

MY MOTHER'S EYES

(1957 - AGED 12)

"Well, he's certainly got your mother's eyes," everyone said about Little Daniel - the final edition to our family, arriving in 1957.

We were still living in East Rudham when Mum went into hospital to have him, but because of her age perhaps, she came down with a bad case of the milk fever and had to stay in a while longer. By the time she came out, the rest of us had already made the move to the new house in High Kelling.

He was a healthy and plump little baby and returned home from the hospital long before Mum did. So despite already having to look after my little sister Valerie, all of a sudden my numerous responsibilities as a 12-year-old girl were doubled.

A new house, a new baby, and no Mum meant it was all hands to the pumps from the very outset - and being new to the village, we didn't know anyone except for the postman. My dad tried to help around the house when he was free, but he was no more use than a chocolate fire poker when it came to babies or housework.

Next door to us lived a couple with no children of their own, Elaine and Keith Murney. Bless them both, they were round our house every day trying to help as best they could. If truth be told, on account of them never having any of their own children, they weren't all that much better than my dad. But between us we struggled through, and even managed to have some laughs along the way.

Bathing time especially, was always an ordeal. Little Daniel certainly wasn't one for the water. Whenever we had him in the kitchen sink he would bawl blue murder. We'd try and get him done quick, one with the soap, one with the towel, the other with the wash cup.

One time, we'd just finished getting him washed and Elaine was there ready with the towel, and as I lifted him free of the sink a sudden jet of water come spurting out of his little winky, just like a fountain. With both my hands holding him, there wasn't much I could do. Instinctively, I turned looking for a place to set him down, but all I did was cause his little jet of wee to spray across the room, and unfortunately all over the front of poor Keith's shirt. Elaine came hurrying over, trying to catch the fountain in the tiny wash cup, but most of it went down the front of her apron. She then slipped on the wet floor and sent the cup flying over the wall.

"Oh, what do I do? What do I do?" she was shrieking as she pulled herself back up.

"The towel. Use the towel!" I said.

"I meant for Daniel," she shrieked.

"So did I! Stop it with the towel!" And then I aimed him straight at her again so she had no choice but to finally smother it.

Where all that piddle had come from, goodness only knows. It was everywhere. All over the sink, all over the kitchen, all over Keith and Elaine. We stood in silence for a moment taking in the scene of devastation.

I was so worried. Not only had I made such a mess, but I'd also caused Elaine to fall over, and then worst of all I'd shouted orders at an adult when all she was trying to do was help. I was certain it would be the very last time they'd come round to help - maybe the last time they would speak to us even.

"Well, blow me down with a feather!" Elaine let out a long breath. "That was a bit exciting, weren't it," and then we all fell about the place in hysterics.

I began to think on it as we were mopping away . . . why hadn't Elaine blown up like what my mother would've done? She didn't even blame me, even though it was clearly my fault. In fact, she'd apologised and helped me clean.

Even with Mum in the hospital, I lived with the fear. Always on edge, always worrying. I could feel her as if she was always there somehow, hovering over me, even in a new house she hadn't yet set foot in.

When Dad told us that she'd been given the all clear, my first thought was, *is everything okay? Is the house clean enough?*

When you're busy, you don't really notice what's around you, but with this news I was able to see the house through my mother's eyes. We had drying nappies hanging everywhere like strings of festival decorations, baby bottles rinsing in the sink, tins of formula milk stacked up on the side, piles of ironed laundry, piles of yet to be ironed laundry - but to name a few. As best I could, I got the house thoroughly cleaned and looking almost normal again. Then I dressed little Daniel in the newest hand-me-down outfit we had. After doing two runs around the house to treble check, I could finally take a moment to step back and see all the work and organising I'd done, and I'm just going to say it - done well. And so, I actually allowed myself to feel proud for once.

Dad of course was in charge of the house in her absence, but there was no doubt about it, it was me who was running the show - little 12-year-old me. Even when Aunt Elaine, Uncle Keith, and my dad were there, I was considered the baby expert amongst us. I was important and I was keeping it all together. I felt like I'd proven myself, passed a test of some sort. I felt that I wasn't so bad anymore. I'd done it, I'd become a good daughter and Mum was going to see that now. It'd been hellish hard work but it was more than worth it to win the love and respect of my own mother.

When I heard the crunch of the car tyres on the gravel, I gave one final look around, straightened the wisps of Daniel's hair and sat him on my lap in the lounge, my knees jiggling away uncontrollably.

"So he's still alive then," she said as she took him from my arms. Nothing more.

I forgave her though, she must've been tired and missing her baby after three months in the hospital.

AUTHOR'S INSIGHT: MY MOTHER'S EYES

As with many of the chapters in the actual novel, I tried to be creative and playful with this chapter's title. Often they have more than one meaning, the true meaning only becoming apparent later on.

In this case, one is initially led to believe *Her Mother's Eyes* is referring to baby Daniel looking similar to their mum. However, by the end, we realise it refers to how the young protagonist desires her mother's validation. The mother is clearly defined as tough to please, and we can read that the protagonist wants nothing more than to do exactly that - please her and gain her respect. This is evident when she tries to view herself and the housework she's done from her mother's perspective - or eyes - in order to assess her success.

Perhaps in more general terms, this piece concerns the differences in perspective brought about by familiarity. The young narrator expects the neighbours, Elaine and Keith, to be angry with the mess and palaver caused by the piddle fountain episode. We can guess that this is exactly how her mother would react in the same situation. But the neighbours are understanding and eventually they laugh about the absurdness of it all. The way we treat our own family often would seem diabolical if we exacted the same treatment on someone we did not share such close familiarity with. Often, the family bond is so deep and strong that we can get away with behaviour that would be viewed unacceptable or too harsh outside of the family context.

Again, the reoccurring theme of this collection arises, concerning responsibility, and the fallibility of adults. The young narrator shows awareness that she is the most capable of the four, despite being the only one who is a child. The adults in this short are almost relegated to being her assistants when it comes to matters of taking care of the baby.

In relation to the novel:

There is a fair amount of subtle irony woven into this chapter that becomes apparent towards the end of the novel - but some of it is too difficult to talk about in detail without giving away too many spoilers!

The main purpose of this chapter was to show Rosie's determination and desire to win her mother's love and respect, as detailed above. So much is asked and expected of her as a 12-year-old child, that it is unfair, yet she shows generous understanding and forgives her mother, an aspect which escalates throughout the full book. A deeper reading could be that actually, she doesn't want to acknowledge harsh truths. Such as, that her mother holds her in such low regard that it borders on resentment. This leads Rosie to hide behind the protective rationale that - her mother's cold and dismissive greeting is only because she *"must've been tired and missing her baby."*

Towards the end of the chapter we begin to realise that winning her mother's respect is perhaps a futile quest, and it begins to raise the crucial question of *why* the mother treats her so badly - what is the mother's motivation or trigger to show such disdain towards her own daughter? It is also begins to foreshadow the mother's unforgiving nature and the ominous presence she casts, even in places that she has yet to set foot.

This chapter was also written with the intention of revealing Rosie's tendency to default to acceptance and subservience. Acceptance that she is to blame for the widdling incident and should take all responsibility for it, as well as the upkeep and condition of the house, and that all these matters should rightly fall upon her tiny shoulders. The subservience is further evident when she worries that by taking control of the situation (including shouting commands at the kindly neighbour), she has somehow broken the hierarchical child - adult system, that a child has no right to be assertive regardless of the situation. But, perhaps crucially, it also shows she has inner strength, confidence, and nous, precisely because she did act, she did take command and delegate, and knew what was the best course of action. It shows us that when situations contrive to back her into a corner, her true self is sometimes revealed, providing a glimpse to her (and of course the reader) of her latent potential, that all is not lost, that she still has the power to affect her future.

4

HOLDING HANDS WITH THE DEVIL

(1958 - AGED 13)

I was always so aware and so worried about my responsibilities of looking after baby Valery - and what's more, I was rarely allowed to forget them. My dad often put the fear of God into me whenever Valerie was poorly. Somehow he always made it feel like it was my fault, such as the time she had a bad case of the croak.

"If anything happens to her..." he said, waving his finger at me, one morning as he left for work.

I did my best, I really did, but that wasn't always good enough. This one time we were blackberry picking on the heath, just on the edge, near where it bordered the Wilson farm. Lil' Pea, already bored of the job in hand, had started to fill his milk tin with dried rabbit pellets instead of berries. I'd finished the heath side of the hedge but still needed to top-off my latest one, so decided to go into the field to get some choice berries from that side.

I checked on Lil' Pea and Puddin, who were as happy as pigs in rabbit poo. Then I checked the field for cattle - empty. So I pushed the pram through the gate and closed it behind us. I made sure to park Valery a little way down, thinking it was best not to leave her too close to the gate in case one of the boys came barrelling through and toppled her over.

I'd worked my way down a fair few yards before topping off the tin. It may sound like a small thing but I got ever so much satisfaction once I'd filled one exactly to the brim - and I wouldn't cheat none, only the finest, darkest blackberries cut the mustard for my tins, whereas Lil' Pea would put any old muck in his, even ones that where still white. But anyway, it had been a successful day so far, so I was feeling happy and begun to hum a nursery rhyme. There'd been no scraped knees, no tears or tantrums, we had plenty of brimming tins, and the rain even looked like it would hold off until we got home. But it's always the way isn't, you just know something bad has to happen when the wind has been blowing in your favour for too long - and so it came to pass. As I glanced up to check on Valerie I got the fright of my life. Where it came from I don't know, but all of a sudden it was there and it had its nose buried right inside the pram. I hurried over, but talked softly.

"Good boy. There's a good boy. Now come on, get out of it now," I was saying.

He slowly lifted his long snout and looked down at me. He had the biggest head I'd ever laid eyes on, and as I went to push it clear he gave a whinnying sneeze. His giant loose lips flapped like a burst inner tube, sending thick white slobber everywhere, with poor little Val taking a direct hit.

Well... I have to say, I did laugh a little as I wiped her face clean, and thankfully, she didn't seem all that bothered by the whole incident. After I pushed the pram further along the hedge, I went back to see him. He was a bloomin great thing, an old black shire horse put out to pasture no doubt. His mane was long and rough and his eyes drooped in a simple but friendly way. To me, the workhorses didn't seem to have the gumption or spirit as the riding horses, but he was loveable enough just the same.

I stroked his thick neck and ran the back of my hand down his forehead all the way to the soft black skin of his nose. I let him eat some grass from my hand, his big rubbery lips tickling my palm. It wasn't the dream horse that galloped through my imagination at night but he was a funny fella and I liked him nonetheless. After he plodded off I went back to fetch the pram.

As I lent over to tuck the blanket back up to Valerie's chin the blood fled my face in an instant. A chill swept through my entire body. My legs went and I nearly pulled the pram down as I scrabbled to get to her. In my mind - she might as well have been holding hands with the devil himself.

Now, growing up in the countryside, you learn from an early age what's what and what's not - and so

I knew, I knew immediately. There was no mistaking what she'd found, what she held between her tiny, pink, chubby fingers.

I was all a-judder as I whipped them away from her, and I was by no means gentle when I desperately hooked a finger inside her mouth, searching all around it. This of course started her bawling, but I had no time for comfort as I tore through the blankets to check there weren't any that'd managed to sneak off and hide amongst the folds - no doubt waiting until later to try and tempt her again.

"Wha's going on?"

I turned to see Lil' Pea leaning his head over the gate.

"You alright Rosie?" he said seeing my face.

"Nothing," I snapped. "Ent nothing."

He peered further over, trying to look what was going on in the pram.

"It's jus' a bee. Fussing near the pram. I just got a bit spooked is all."

"A bee?"

"Yes. That's what I said, dint I."

I don't harbour much, if any, hate in me, and especially for things that can't help it such as plants, but I made a special case for deadly nightshade after that day. I mean, why does nature even need a berry so dangerous? What would be wrong with *delicious* nightshade? I think what I hated most was how underhand it was, how it's little star-shaped leaves - like a pixie's collar - was trying to attract curious little minds. How it appeared as you friend at first, but it wouldn't be until too late that you learnt its true intentions.

I was checking on Val every second as we made our way home. My heart skipping overtime.

"Why you keep fussing on her? You thinking she may've got stung?"

"No! No, she didn't get stung. She's just fine, alright." Then I made sure Lil' Pea and Puddin knew not to say anything of the bee once we got in. "We don't want to worry no one unnecessarily now, do we?" Or at least not worry anyone else, cos I for one couldn't sleep a wink that night.

Every minute, I was jumping out of bed to go check on her. Peering through the darkness, checking her chest was still moving and that she hadn't turned blue in the face.

The next week, when we went back to the heath, I pointed out the plant to the other kids to make sure they knew about it. Then I gave it what for with a stick, first cutting it down, then hacking it up, before finally stomping it into the ditch good and proper.

"There." I said, dusting off my hands like I'd seen my dad do after a job well done.

The boys stood staring at me - open mouthed, as if I was some sort of loon.

"It's a bad, bad plant is all," I said to my audience. "And don't you forget it."

AUTHOR'S INSIGHT: HOLDING HANDS WITH THE DEVIL

This piece also follows the common themes of this collection in regards to the protagonist feeling the heavy weight of responsibility always resting on her young shoulders, and perhaps asks if it is fair to bestow such burdens on a child? Just as the proverb of the scorpion and the frog goes, a child cannot help acting like a child, no matter what expectations are put upon them and their resolve to adhere to them – it's in their nature. In this case, the child in Rosie is engaged by the sudden appearance of a horse, she can't help herself but to momentarily forget the adult expectations foisted upon her, and she reverts to her natural, curious child-like state. But as always, unfortunately for her it only takes one moment, one slip for it all to go wrong once more.

In fact, it seems the harder she tries the more matters are likely to take a turn for the worse. She states herself, in this piece, that she is acutely aware of her responsibility and how seriously it must be taken. She even shows the forethought of predicting where the danger may come from when she decides to position the pram away from the gate to prevent a rambunctious younger brother toppling it over. However, as is her curse, once again in doing what she perceives as the correct course of action, she inadvertently places baby Valery closer to the deadly night shade berries.

Ultimately, there is a glimmer of hope for her offered in this piece however. We see this when despite the repeated misfortune that plagues her, she still has the capacity to learn and to recognise a level of responsibility in teaching the other children of the dangers. She shows them the bush and then proceeds to destroy it to prevent it endangering anyone else.

In relation to the novel:

On a surface level, this piece reinforces Rosie's love of horses and the fear their dad holds over the children. But it also shows us the pressure she is under and the expectations she constantly has to deal with, and often with little in the way of gratitude. Rather than being praised for how well she continuously looks after the three young children, she is more likely to be met with threats, which only make her more nervous and therefore likely to make mistakes.

Another aspect this chapter was intended to convey is how unaware her younger siblings are of most of the things going on around them. They are free from responsibility and worries, they can fill their tins with unripe berries, they can even stop and play, be silly and fill them with rabbit poop instead – something that would be unthinkable for Rosie to do. Yet, the one moment in which Rosie relaxes and shows any kind of natural child-like behaviour - petting the horse – it all goes wrong. This chapter was designed to help sew this theme of her baring everything herself, of feeling isolated and alone, that she is the only one suffering, that she can't let anyone else in or expect them to understand her situation. This is developed further, throughout the novel, until it escalates into far more serious issues. The intention was for this early chapter to sow the seed of this from the outset, and again as is a common motif, how bad things can grow from poison seeds and become far bigger, far-reaching problems if left to grow unchecked.

5

THE BAMFORD TWINS

(1960 ~ AGED 15)

[Content Warning: This chapter contains an old-fashioned racial epithet and a graphic description of violence.]

Pam Linga-Linga-Low-Low wasn't the only evacuee my mother took in during the war. There was also the two young twins, Ron and Bob Bamford - a couple of handsome boys and no mistake. And again, like Pam, they too came back for visits when they were all grown up and the war was all but done with.

Their father ran a car garage, so the boys were surrounded by motors from a very young age. Bob, as a promising young talent, eventually went on to become a racing-car driver. He liked to come visit us so he could unwind in the countryside every now and then. Whereas Ron, who loved the cars just a much but didn't quite share the talents of his twin, decided to take a different path through life. He'd been fascinated by World War Two as a kid, and so he joined the army as soon as he was old enough. However, it wasn't soon enough for him to be able to see any action beyond the army training base.

The first time he came back to stay with my family was with his new wife for their honeymoon, then the odd holiday after that. Then in '56 he finally got what he'd always wanted and was sent out to serve his country in the Suez War. But unfortunately, life has a dark ol' sense of humour, or doesn't have one at all, because he never came back - that is to say, the *real* Ron never came back.

You see, during the fighting, he went through quite the terrible experience, and it changed him, and I mean completely changed him - even the way he looked, can you believe. You could still see that the handsomeness was once there, but all the nerves in his face had gone, to the extent you'd no longer think him and his brother were siblings - let alone twins. However, it was the personality change that was most troubling, and I hate to say it but he turned into a right nasty bugger at times. His wife struggled to cope with the man who'd returned in place of her beloved husband, and so she'd send him down to stay with us, just so she could get a bit of badly needed respite.

He told me once what had done it for him. Now, I'm gonna tell it just as he told it, and I know it ent right anymore to say it, but these were his words. He said, how one time during the fighting this wog fella came at his friend. He said it all happened so fast and so close that he was left with no choice but to use his bayonet. He said he'd never wanted to do it, but it had to be done and done proper.

"And so I stuck him, stuck him through. Right into his belly it went," he said. "And then I just kept pushing until his feet were almost lifted off the ground."

He said he could feel the poor fella's pulse juddering down through the blade, down through the gun's wooden stock, that he could feel the knock and scrape of the metal barrel on bones, ribs, and whatever else. And ever since that day, he didn't like doing things with his hands much anymore. Anytime he did, he said he could feel it all over again, like his hands had their own memory - yet the only thing they wanted to remember was that god awful feeling.

I watched him clench his thumbs inside his fists, then rub his fingers against each other, then down his sides as he winced and grimaced at the retelling of his own grisly story. He said he couldn't stop himself from hearing the noises it made too, as the blade squished its way in.

"Then, there was some kinda problem. You see, it'd gone in too far," he said. "And I couldn't get it out again. So I was pulling . . . kept pulling it, pulling it so hard that both me and the wog fella were screaming blue murder. But it just wouldn't budge . . ." Then he drifted away for a second or two, his face contorting.

He said, in the end they told him the only way to

free his gun was to fire it off. And this is what he did. And this is what *did* him.

"They train you ever so hard in the army," he said. "They make you run and jump and climb like there's no tomorrow. Make you clean your kit, as if a baby needed to eat off it. But you know something that there wasn't any training for? There weren't no training for taking another human's life. For seeing their face, seeing their blood, *hearing* their blood bubbling and rattling in their lungs, hearing their screams, then . . . then the nothingness . . . " he said, eyes drifting to floor.

"They just go silent. And they're gone. And I don't mean like the lights have just been snuffed out, I mean everything, everything they were, every memory and thought they ever had . . . gone. And all you can do is just watch as their body becomes, well, just a . . . a . . . thing. And all that you're aware of is your own heart thumping through your chest, as if in sympathy for the one you've stopped. And all you can do is look down at him, laying there, absolutely still. So much life suddenly come to an end, suddenly becoming no more than an object. And the only thing you really know is - *I did that*. I made that object, with my own hands. It was my doing."

After he finished speaking he didn't move. He sat there, eyes fixed on the floor in front of him. I didn't know whether I should say something, whether I should go fetch someone. In the end I just got up and crept away. Maybe it weren't the right thing to do, but I didn't know what else I could or should do.

My mum was much better with him than I was. There was no doubting he was in a sorry state, but he quickly became a difficult man to like - I'd even go as far to say he developed a right nasty streak. On one occasion, I got up for work and went to get my bike out of the shed, only to find he'd done both my tires in with a knife. Heaven knows why, since he hated using his hands, and surely wasn't keen on using knives no more. Even though it deeply shames me to say it, I can't say I weren't relieved to see him go each time he packed up his bag and returned to his poor wife.

AUTHOR'S INSIGHT: THE BAMFORD TWINS

Much darker in tone, this piece explores the naivety and follies of youth, echoing the timeless proverb of *be careful what you wish for*. In Ron's inexperienced young mind, serving one's country and fighting in a war seems honourable and perhaps glamorous. His brother becomes a racing-car driver, an exciting sport in which one can often be projected as a hero. We could presume that Ron didn't quite share the same attributes as his brother in order to match his success. But maybe the passion to achieve, or to test oneself was still innate. Does this lead him to search for something with a lower bar of entry, but a similar opportunity for glory? Then along comes the army, always hungry for young men, and this satisfies the need or lack that Ron so acutely feels.

Similar to the other shorts, this is about a young person learning the often harsh truths of life. Ron surely knew that if his dream of fighting in a war was to be realised, it would involve death and maybe require him to kill, but he soon learns there is no glamour in killing. To further compound it, the suggestion is that he was sold on a dream but not adequately warned or prepared for the reality, and we could read into it that he feels he's been abandoned afterwards. There's no mention of counselling, and even his wife struggles to be with him, and wants to be away from him at times. He has to resort to unloading his trauma to a 15-year-old girl who only seems to be listening through politeness. Then finally, even she abandons him, leaving him sat alone in the room, staring at the floor with only his torment for company.

This short also highlights the lack of support available for those whose countries ask so much of them, and perhaps even the lack of awareness/recognition back then, of the impact of PTSD. Ron is cognisant of the existence and cause of his post-traumatic stress. But even though he can recognise it himself, it is no less debilitating or no less of a struggles to manage - seen in the rather bleak denouement when he damages the narrator's bicycle for no apparent reason. And to further compound it, he uses a knife with his own hands, a manner which he earlier proclaims causes him great pain and suffering.

In relation to the novel:

This was also difficult to remove, as I feel it subtly serves the overall story in many ways. Again the symbolic motif of poisoned seeds bearing poisoned fruit is evident. It reinforces that "bad" people aren't born bad, that usually life and unfortunate circumstances lead them down that road. Everyone has their reasons, has their story.

Another purpose of this chapter was to raises the stakes for Rosie by showing the dangers of how trauma can cause irreversible effects later in life. Also the risk of being careful of what you wish for, as it might just come true - something Rosie struggles with as the novel progresses. As she gains more experience of life and learns more of its secrets, the prospect of following her mother's path starts to become a horrifying and seemingly inescapable reality, rather than an aspirational childhood dream.

It can also be seen that when Ron talks of a person becoming no more than an object in death (though of course literally in this chapter), this resonates metaphorically with how Rose feels later in the novel when she begins to lose her sense of being and self worth. She starts to feel as if she is no more than an empty husk of a person, only a shell.

Again the chapter title, *The Bamford Twins*, can be read in different ways. Literally, as there were two brothers, or figuratively in referring to the two sides of Ron - the one before, and the one after the tragic incident that irrevocably changed him.

6

ALL HELL'S HOOVES

(1958 ~ AGED 13)

Just up the way from our house there was a large cattle farm, and every week or so the cattle would need to be moved to fresh pastures. When this was done, the young farm boys would simply open up the gate and send in the dogs. A few minutes later, all hell would break loose as they came thundering out. It was not just the cows but the heavy horses too. The farm boys never did give any thought to what might be coming up the way . . . cars, cyclists, or even a young girl pushing a pram with two little'uns in tow.

And I tell yuh, when all hell's hooves poured down one of them high-hedged Norfolk lanes, it left no escape for anyone caught in their way. It was but for a stroke of God-sent luck that there happened to be a gap in the hedge that allowed us to duck out of the way in time - no easy matter with a pram, you can be sure of that.

I gave them three pieces of my mind when the

boys came laughing down the road afterwards. But they just looked at me, didn't say a word, carried on like I weren't there or hadn't even spoke, like we didn't even matter. That just seemed to be how things were, nothing was thought to be dangerous until it went wrong and some poor bugger got hurt. I know most people nowadays moan about things being too far the other way, *health and safety gone mad*, and all that, but I know which makes more sense to me. Back then, people seemed more ready to just accept bad occurrences as part and parcel of life.

It's hard to say, but it makes you wonder if the war affected the way people thought. Was it just a case that everyone was loosening their belts and breathing out a big sigh, that nothing else seemed that serious or worth worrying about anymore? Or with all that death and destruction that went on, did it make lives seem cheaper? Or did it make people more selfish upon realising how fragile life could be, so they thought they should concentrate mostly on themselves, even at the expense of other people's safety? Or was this just me overthinking things again?

It wasn't exactly like the wild-west, there did still seem to be respect for people in authority, like your teachers, doctors, and policemen types. There was an incident with our doctor that really stuck with me and made me think on things. It was when we were all young and my brother Billy still had time for his annoying kid sister. We were sat on the back lawn cutting things out for a scrapbook, when Karl came out of the house in a rush. As he passed by, he gave Billy a whack round the back of the head. Being boys close in age, those two were always at each other. Winding one another up, like a game. The first to get uppity and start the fight was the loser, no matter who won the actual fight - which was usually Karl.

I don't know where it came from, because me and Billy were happy as Larry sitting there doing our cutting, but Billy just reacted. In an instant, the scissors flew from his hand and stuck right into Karl's back.

It took all of us, even Billy, a second or two to realise what had actually happened. Then it all went off.

Karl was shouting and screaming in a panic. I shot up and ran yelling for help. And Billy . . . Billy just sat there cross-legged, all quiet, his face as white as snow.

There were men working on the paths nearby who came and took him to the doctors. Luckily the scissors hadn't gone in too far and had stuck mostly into the fat of his back. He had a couple of stitches but not much more.

The doctor brought Karl and Mum home that day, and then asked to speak to Billy alone. He led him down the garden out of sight, reminding me of the time Dad walked the same route with the newborn kittens in a hessian sack. Everyone was quiet, not really sure what to say or what was gonna to happen.

Unlike the kittens though, Billy did come back.

He never told me what was said, but he and Karl never got rowing again after that day. There's often been times in my life when I've wanted to know so badly what was said, wanting to know how just a few words could be so powerful.

AUTHOR'S NOTE: ALL HELL'S HOOVES

This piece again covers the theme of responsibility relating to children and growing up, but I won't go into that again. It also concerns the juncture in a child's life when they begin to learn or realise that the world can be a dangerous place, that safety and security are not a given or a right. That danger can in fact come from somewhere completely unexpected, like a cattle stampede down a narrow country lane, or from a seemingly innocuous incident with your own sibling. When a child becomes aware of their own (and other's) mortality, it can be can be a monumental, difficult, and defining moment in their life.

It also briefly touches on how society had to recalibrate after the devastation of a world war. After such an unprecedented and far-reaching event, the pre-war way of life could not immediately return. It was a time for readjustments as people tried to get back to what they considered normal. And how much of this becomes sown into the fabric of society and pervades the life of those whose generation didn't even directly experienced the war? Can preceding world events affect a child's behaviour, such as Billy's, who would have likely not have been directly conscious of the war? Would he still have thrown the sharp scissors into his own brother's back without the influence and presence of the war on society as a whole?

This piece also comments on the fact that war brought the best out in people too. Could another side effect be that people were more likely to be altruistic towards those in trouble? The men working on the nearby path dropped tools and came to the aid of a kid hurt in a silly sibling quarrel. The doctor goes beyond his usual expected duties, by taking the kid home and trying to solve the cause/origin of the injury - the sibling rivalry, rather than just being content with helping fix the result of it. Perhaps after a war and having witnessed how quickly simple things can escalate, there is greater motivation to mediate in order to stop further conflict.

In relation to the novel:

Again, this reveals some of Rosie's potential. Her awareness of danger and the responsibilities that people should take more seriously. But also, much in the same way as the previous chapter, when pushed, she does have the potential to push back. She remonstrates with the boys, perhaps so much so they have no answer or comeback to offer and therefore choose to ignore her.

This chapter was also written with the intention of conveying a slight edge to the world that the novel is set in, that things weren't always safe and (excuse the pun) rosy warm. It served to prepare the reader for the more serious and darker aspects of the novel that begin to materialise in the latter half.

Finally, Rosie is left wondering if there is some magic that she's not privy to that could or would solve all her problems. If words alone can stop a squabbling war between two brothers that has been going on their whole lives, surely words have powers untold. This chapter shows us that she reached such a seemingly hopeless and desperate point in life that she was even prepared to look for an unknown and maybe unlikely remedy - all in hopes of finding a magic cure for her ever-escalating problems.

7

NIGHT MANOEUVRES

(1959 ~ AGED 14)

I ent afraid of the dark. Never was, never have been. After all, it ent the darkness that hurts you, it's only the monsters that hide within it. But that ent to say there weren't times when it happened to be dark and I managed to get myself scared. I remember one particular night, deep into autumn, a night darker than most with the fickle moon having buggered off on one of its regular flings. The hazy scent of summer had long gone and in its place was the smell of damp earth and rotting chestnut husks. I remember everything being so quiet and still, not even a stir of wind. And once again I found myself hiding on the edge of those blasted woods with just the *tick - tick - tick* of the rusted pocket-watch to keep me company.

As usual, I was in my nightdress, my brother's wellies, and my mother's coat. Unlike me, my mum was a gret ol' girl, so the sleeves hung way down past my hands. The best I could do to keep them out of reach of the nagging brambles below, was to hug them around myself. I wasn't scared at this point though. You see, this was a fairly normal way for me, aged 14, to be spending my evening.

Mostly I was just bored. Bored - of - waiting. Occasionally, I squelched my feet into the guck of leaves to ease the ache in the back of my legs. And also cos it made a funny noise.

Little Miss Muffet sat on her tuffet . . .

I liked to recite nursery rhymes when I was alone - just to pass the time, mind you. But because we couldn't have anyone knowing I was there, hiding in those woods, the words always stayed silent prisoners inside my head.

. . . eating her curds and . . . and I knew I wasn't alone, even before I first heard them coming my . . .

. . . whey . . .

I ent sure how. You know what it's like sometimes - you just get *that* feeling.

Then along came . . . a . . . s . . . spi-

CRICK.

-der.

I stopped and I listened.

With it not being my first time in those woods, I'd learnt how to pick out the natural noises, such as the creaking of branches or the gossiping of leaves in a breeze, from those unnatural, such as a body breaking through foliage or an animal rooting around in the undergrowth. And so I knew this wasn't no crunch of twigs under a dog walker's feet, or a hedgehog snuffling through the dead leaves. It was a different kind of noise. A kind that sent an army of insects with tiny, sharp, prickling feet creeping their way up my arms. A kind that tightened my breath by wringing at my lungs. A kind that caused a slow tumbling and turning to wallow up from the pit of my belly, up, up, up into my chest. For this was a far more disturbing kind of noise. More disturbing, because it was the noise of something trying its hardest *not* to be heard.

After another *CRICK,* came a long drawn out rustle.

Then a sound to the right.

Then another - this time from the left.

And again. And again. My head snapped towards each one. One here, one there, one near, one far, one . . . everywhere. All around me. Too many to count. Too many to keep track of.

By now the panic was pumping through my blood and pounding in my eardrums. The undergrowth, painted black by shadow, started to twitch as if a dark and deadly rainstorm was sweeping towards me. Closer and closer, creeping and crawling it came.

A thousand thoughts crowded my mind, all fighting and colliding against each other. *Should I shout? Should I scream? Should I run? Should I hide? If I run - which way? Should I scream while I run? Or better to save my energy?* But fast thoughts are a friend to no one when your legs ent even listening. And so . . . I simply did nothing. I was frozen to the spot. Frozen by what I call a moment of uncertain—certainty. Uncertain *what* was happening, but certain I was *about* to find out.

Right before it did happen, there was a moment of calm, a moment of perfect stillness as the silence wrapped itself around me. I took a sharp breath, which steadfast refused to come out again. And I waited.

It started with a short, sharp bark. On its command, broken, dark figures rose out of the ground like the waking dead. They came from everywhere, loping out of the gloom with their huge misshapen heads. Their tentacles and antennas flailing wildly. Shouts and roars bounced and crashed through the trees as they bore down upon me. It was as if the very forest itself had come alive and wanted to gobble me up.

There ent no denying that I was fearing, but very quickly something else took over. It's hard to describe with my words, but I remember thinking, *Oh well, so this is happening then, let's just get on with it shall we.* I guess I can only say it was a kind of acceptance. An acceptance that comes from realising you are powerless. Realising you can't change things, that all you can really do is wait, and hope. Just hope that things will turn out for the best - eventually.

In all fairness, the sergeant was ever so apologetic when he realised I was but a young girl. Mind, that didn't stop him from scolding me for troshin around in dark all on my own, but then he apologised again for scolding me. He then said they'd escort me home, but I told him I was waiting for my mum and could they be sure not to give her a fright, should they cross her path.

Each young recruit was then made to file past and mumble a sheepish apology before they went back to running round the countryside playing at being in the army.

I had a little chuckle as I watched them march down the road - with the ferns, twigs, and broken branches that they'd stuck in their helmets and buttonholes, wobbling and bobbling away. It made them look more like a troupe of circus clowns than a troop of soldiers.

But their peculiar shapes quickly melted into the blackness, and soon even the *clip-clop* of their marching boots was swallowed by the night, and I was left alone once more.

And so I went back to waiting for my mother in those blasted woods. Waiting to see her familiar ambling frame emerge from the darkness, waiting for her to comeback from wherever it was that she had spent her evening, waiting - just like a good little girl should.

Tick - tick - tick.

AUTHOR'S INSIGHT: NIGHT MANOEUVRES

This piece touches on the power of the imagination to create fear and how the mind works to explain unknown situations - often with extreme and unrealistic exaggeration. Although the fear emanates from something real, and Rosie is savvy and has previous experience of this situation, her imagination still conjures up a scenario in which the forest is trying to consume her and that monsters with antennae are hunting her.

Again there is the running theme of this short story collection regarding the fallibility of adults and the common notion or perception held by children that adults are almost godlike and should always be obeyed. That adults are a perfectly formed, functioning humans that do no wrong and make no mistakes. When in reality, we all know we are far from perfect and that becoming a complete, faultless person is a constant journey to an impossible destination.

In this piece, this is represented by the fact that the sergeant in charge of the army recruits, ends up stalking and jumping out on a young girl by herself in a forest. No thought is given to the shock, or even trauma it could cause her. Further more, it's confirmed in the final paragraph that the girl is waiting for her mother, and we realise that it was her mother who instructed her to wait there - alone and in the dark. Of course the girl accepts this, as obeying adults is what *"good little girls"* should do. Ultimately, it could be judged that the most adult-like behaviour is actually exhibited by the young girl, despite her penchant for reciting nursery rhymes and imagining monsters. After all, she has the forethought to ask the sergeant to be careful not to scare her mother if they cross her path too.

On a deeper level, this short can be seen as a metaphor for growing up, transitioning from a child who is scared of monsters under the bed, to an adolescent who has real-world responsibilities and real fears to consider. This is reinforced by the changing of seasons from the *"hazy scent of summer long gone"* which represents the warmth, comfort, and nostalgia of childhood, to *"the smell of damp earth and rotting chestnut husks"* of autumn and the realisation that life isn't just made up of sunny pleasant days. The reality of life begins to set in. Maybe not quite as harsh as winter yet (and full adulthood), but the realisation that not everything is as easy and as carefree as the majority of children's lives should ideally be. The *"tick-tick-ticking"* pocket watch also representing the transition and the passing of time.

In relation to the full novel:

For a very long time, this last story of this book, was actually the prologue of the novel, *Goodbye to Ribbons*. I agonised over the opening sentence and paragraph of this chapter many times, only to eventually take the very hard decision to remove it completely. I like it as a piece of writing, but whilst it informs the countryside setting, introduces many of the novel's themes and motifs, and raises questions of intrigue, tonally it just didn't feel right in places to be the opening chapter. In fact, one early beta-reader (at that point not knowing any context of the novel) initially thought I was writing a zombie book! Maybe that will be my next one, haha!

The motifs it sets up, and that still remain in the full novel, include the rusted pocket watch, the flights of fantasy, and the reciting of nursery rhymes during times of stress. This chapter also contains some useful metaphors for some of the themes of the novel, such as when she talks about acceptance and feeling powerless, which relates to her resignation when her attempts to be more proactive in changing her life always seem to fail.

Again the title, *Night Manoeuvres,* has more than one meaning, as it could apply to the army practice but also a nod to the regular evening arrangements the protagonist, Rosie, has with her mother as well as an insinuation of what the mother is actually getting up to, while her young daughter patiently waits for her in the dark forest *"just like a good little girl should."* And the final image serves as a nice metaphor for an integral part of the novel. That of the army (usually the good guys, the people who are supposed to help and be heroes) disappearing, leaving her, alone, abandoning her if you like, before her mother (who you may have realised already, is one of the main antagonists) emerges from the darkness, a foreboding presence perhaps, coming to get her...

Well, there we go. I hope you enjoyed this collection of short stories, and if you did, please consider taking a look at the full novel ***Goodbye to Ribbons by W.S. Ishida*** *(that's me) which is based on a true story.*

In the novel, you can follow Rosemary's journey from the age of 3 to 38 as she reflects back (now at the age of 65 years old) on the tumultuous events and resulting scars from the extraordinary life she lived.

Please be warned that the novel contains themes that are much stronger than those present in this short-story collection.

Further Reading

Goodbye to Ribbons is a historical novel set deep in the rural British countryside at the close of WWII. It follows the journey of Rosemary Page as she navigates the traumatic waters of the oppressive relationships that threaten to destroy her. Just as she begins to grasp onto the edges of hope, matters take a shocking turn with the discovery of a family secret she wishes she'd never been exposed to.

Goodbye to Ribbons is poetic, funny, and occasionally gut-wrenchingly brutal - but ultimately an uplifting tale with a real emotional heart that will live with you long after the final page.

Available from Amazon on Kindle, in Paperback, and in Large Print.

GOODBYE TO RIBBONS

W.S. ISHIDA

~Based on a true story, a powerful and thought-provoking novel, set deep in rural Britain after the close of WWII~

Goodbye to Ribbons

PROLOGUE

AGED 65 (2010)

I wouldn't ever say it's easy watching a person die, no matter what the circumstances. But it's also hard for me to say that there wasn't a part of me that was glad when he did. Well, maybe glad ain't quite right, but I never have been that good with getting my thoughts down. Me, I prefer to talk.

Actually, I've been talking to one of them psychiatrist people, would you believe. She's actually quite nice. I like her. She listens to me. In fact, she was the one who said I should do this—you know, write it all down, like a proper story.

Mostly, she listens with her legs crossed, leaning forwards, head cocked to one side and her thin eyebrows raised. Sometimes she nods along, and sometimes she asks me questions too.

"And how does that make you feel now?" she might say.

Or, "If that were to happen today, what would you

think, or how would you react? In fact, tell me, what would the Rosemary sitting here now, say to the Rosemary back then?"

But my answer is always the same. Okay, I'm slowly losing the use of my hands, what with the rheumatoid arthritis, and walking isn't getting any easier, but I got my own house, my own husband, two little dogs and a fair few friends. In fact, every summer we have a big party here in the garden—which if you'll forgive me for being a braggart—is slowly becoming quite the event on some people's calendars.

So I gotta say, I'm happy. And if I changed any one little thing from my past, then who's to say I would've even got to where I am now.

Yeah, things did go—if you'll 'scuse my French—horribly tits up for a long, long while, but here I am. And, there was even one or two laughs that were had along the way, so you know what—I'll take that.

Anyway, listen to me waffling on already and I haven't even got started. Now, I do want to say one final thing —please be warned, I'm gonna tell it how it was, warts and all. And I ent gonna pull any punches, so to speak, that just isn't me. So, if you care to listen, here it is. This is my story from the very beginning.

1

THE GOOD LITTLE GIRL

AGED 3 (1948)

If I only had one thing going for me throughout my life, it was being as tough as a pair of old leather boots that'd been left out in the rain too long. You see, I'd quietly put up with things that most others wouldn't. And so even though they thought I might never walk again, I listened and I did as I was told—just like a good little girl should.

"Keep your head up and always look forward," they kept telling me, when at 3 years old I had to learn to walk for the second time in my life.

And it wasn't long before I was able to straighten my knees. And a short while after that, hobble about with the help of a frame. Then, after five long bedridden-months spent alone in a dark room, the day eventually came when it was all over and I could once again stand on my own two feet.

The old clothes peg was finally removed from the curtains and the lights turned on. I was jiggling with excitement knowing that I was going to be with my family again, that I was going home. They dressed me up in the clothes I came in with, the only ones that weren't hospital issue. Then I waited.

I remember it so clearly, sitting on that bed. The sunshine warming my back. My pale skinny legs swinging free as the excitement tickled away at the inside of my belly.

I heard her first—a distant voice booming through the corridors. Then there was the odd moment of silence, which was when the staff got their turn to speak before she started up again.

My legs stopped swinging.

"Uh yes, she's just in here, we urm—"

But before they could finish, in she stomped. A big-bosomed, bolshie woman with waves of thick, light-brown hair and the most striking red lipstick you ever did see. She stood towering over me, swamped in a lavish fox-fur coat, hands on hips.

My tiny fingers gripped at the bedsheet.

"Right. Come on then. We ent got all day," she said with a weariness, as if we'd already outstayed our welcome.

I didn't reply.

I didn't even move.

"Come on. Let's not hang about. Don't want to keep these busy people waiting, do yuh."

I looked to the doctor, who gave me a nod and an over-practiced smile. But all I could do was pull the sheet up from the bed and hold it in front of my face, my eyes barely peeping over the top. The doctor looked to the woman and then back to me. He wanted to say something but clearly wasn't sure of himself. She often had that effect on people.

"It's... it's just your mother, she's come to take you home, Rosemary. You... you do want to go home, don't you?"

Of course I wanted to go home, more than anything in the world. However, something just didn't feel right.

All I can think of now, is perhaps the picture I'd built up in my mind over those last five months wasn't marrying-up to the one who stood towering over me there and then.

2

EARLIEST MEMORIES

People often like to ask what your earliest memory is, but how can we ever really be sure. It's always so hazy when you're young, and then of course you have other people's memories and their stories thrown into the mix. Then soon enough things get all clouded up and before you know it you're not really sure you can believe your own mind anymore.

I was only 3 years old when I went to stay at that small hospital in Cromer. I don't remember all that much before it. It was the rheumatic fever that landed me there, so I was told. They reckon I got it by absorbing dampness up through my knees while playing in the sand heap. And so at the age most kids were getting to master their legs, I went back to being pushed around in a pram.

I remember my hospital room always being so gloomy.

"We told you already, the light's no good for it,"

they'd say as they re-fastened the curtains. But the curtains didn't just keep the light out, but also any chance of having company in the empty bed next to mine. After all, who in their right mind would be able to handle being shut away like that in the darkness every hour of the waking day.

Occasionally they'd wheel me down Cromer Pier for some fresh air, and that would be as much as I saw of the outside world for a good while. They'd push me along, the wheels *buddum, buddumming* across the wooden slats all the way to the very end. I mostly liked to watch the gulls wheeling through the sky. Their cries blocking out the heavy sighs of the sea coming up through the slats, as it swayed non-stop back and forth between the pier's dark stained legs.

Looking out at the sea caused me to have funny feelings at times. I didn't like the way it went on forever and ever, how there was no end in sight. A nurse once told me not to worry, that even though I couldn't see it yet, if I kept going I'd eventually get to Holland.

"And you know something else, if you just keep on going without ever changing your course, you'll go all the way around and eventually end up exactly where you started from," she said smiling down at my unblinking face. "Now isn't that something to think about."

3

THE PUB SINGER

I never had no fancy dreams like the other kids of being a movie star, a singer, an astronaut or even a famous figure skater. All I ever wanted was to be like my mother. And for her to like me.

"Salt of the earth she is," they'd say.

"Do anything for anyone," others would tell me.

"A real good'un, and that's not for arguing with."

Everybody loved her, and even in the small town of East Rudham where I spent most of my childhood, *everybody* was a whole lot of people, so I had no choice but to believe it. But if that was the truth, it left me with only one answer—that it was me, that I was the problem.

I was born on Monday the 1st of May 1945, the day after Hitler killed himself and the day before the German forces in Italy surrendered. With the war all but done, there was a positivity in the air and a feeling of a new beginning for most folks.

When I arrived into the world I already had two older brothers, Karl and Billy, and another three brothers and a sister still to come. We grew up in a tiny village deep in the Norfolk countryside—all of us crammed into a busy council house that seemed to shrink every year.

We were lucky to have a bit of a garden. With seven kids under one roof, it acted like the release spout on our disgruntled pressure cooker that would rattle away on top of the paint-chipped stove. The garden was split into two by a row of conifers, and although both bits were at the rear of the house we still called them the front garden and the back garden. The "front garden" being the grassy lawn right outside the back door. Most of this was taken up by the junk-filled shed and the two old caravans—where we stored all the junk that we couldn't fit in the shed. Behind the conifers was the "back garden" where we had the old veg patch, the compost heap, the bonfire pit and then at the very end our rather unique double outhouse that my dad built with his own two hands.

The back garden was mostly where you'd find my dad, Trevor. It was a place he could get away from it all and go for a quiet smoke. He was a tall, rangy man, not much one for words, preferring a grunt if he could get away with it. His face thin and weathered, as were his hands that never seemed to scrub up much better than grimy. He worked his whole life as a farm labourer but wore a shirt and waistcoat to work every single day, as well as his beige flat cap that hid his thinning light-brown hair. Despite being as quiet as a dormouse hiding from a cat, I always knew when he was at home by the familiar smell of stale tobacco smoke and faint whiff of oil. Everything was kept well oiled at our house, there was never a squeak or groan to be heard from hinge nor spindle. In fact, there were only four things I ever remember seeing in his hands. If he was outdoors, it was a rolled-up cigarette and the narrow-spouted oilcan. If he was indoors, it was the newspaper. And if one of us kids had got wrong, it was the old leather belt that despite my best efforts I was no stranger to.

By no stretch of the imagination was I a naughty kid—none of us were, really. We never set out to do anything bad, never had no ill-intentions, yet the belt still managed to find the back of our legs on a regular basis. I feared my dad but never blamed him for the punishments. I was always able to see our blame in the matters. I soon understood that if something got broke, even accidentally, then someone got the belt. Sometimes, it would be everyone who happened to be in the room of the wrongdoing, that way he knew the real culprit wouldn't get away with it. But a day or two after the pain had faded, it was forgotten and things carried on as normal like they always did.

Later in my childhood, when I was able to process things better, there was one thing I couldn't forget, one thing that I struggled to get past, and that was the way I'd treated my mum the day she came to pick me up from the hospital. I cursed myself for it because I could only think this was the reason, this was the cause, this was the seed from where it all started. How must it have felt, to be shunned in front of all those people by her own flesh and blood, by a being that she made, that came from her, that was part of her? But little did I know, or could I've known, the poisoned seed had already been sown before my existence had even come to be.

I tried my damnedest to make things right and win back her love—that famous love that all others got so easily and for free. I accepted it was my fault and forgave her time and time again for the way she was and the things she said, the things she did. I lied for her, betraying myself and my own family. I even covered for her when she didn't have the will or the want to do it for herself. I gave her everything and got nothing back, and all cos I accepted the blame. But for some reason, what I never thought about was that in those five months that her infant daughter had been sick in the hospital, my marvellous mother hadn't visited her once.

Back Cover

How much would you sacrifice, betray, and forgive for just a few scant crumbs of much-needed love?

Growing up in the Norfolk countryside at the end of WWII, shy and prone to flights of fantasy, Rosemary Page only wants one thing ~ to be exactly like her well-loved mother. That is until the truth begins to emerge and her dream threatens to become her inescapable destiny.

Rosie must decide how many morals she is willing to sacrifice, how much cruelty she is willing to tolerate, and how many lies she is willing to tell to prevent her family from being torn apart at the very seams.

However, when the confident and brash, Teddy Miller, falls off the back of a motorbike and into Rosie's life, he proves to be the only person willing to stand up for her. But as a slave to his emotions, does he simply love her too much to be the saviour she so desperately craves?

Often beautiful, sometimes brutal, but always page turning ~ you have been warned.

Praise for Goodbye to Ribbons

"This book had me gripped. I didn't want to stop reading for anything or anyone. Brilliantly written."

5-star review - Judith (UK)

"This is a highly readable, deeply touching and thought provoking book. I'd recommend it to anyone seeking a life affirming read, or something to inspire courage."

5-star review - Amazon customer (UK)

"A captivating story about the resilience of the human spirit"

5-star review - Kari (USA)

"...a well written thought provoking book. I will be recommending it to my book club for their next read."

5-star review - Margaret (USA)

"Read in one sitting. A powerful and engrossing story."

5-star review - Cleo (UK)

"I feel like I've been on a journey! Heart breaking, insightful and a damn good book."

5-star review - Simon B (UK)

FINAL NOTE FROM THE AUTHOR

If you enjoyed these first few chapters of my novel, you can discover more from my author's website **wsishida.com**

And if you really, really enjoyed this short story collection and/or the novel, please feel free to leave a star-rating or review on your preferred website such as Amazon or Goodreads. Reviews and ratings help other people discover my writing, as well as supporting my author career and my aspirations to write many more books.

With thanks,

W.S. Ishida

SOCIAL MEDIA

If you would like to follow the author on social media it can be done so at the following places:

Facebook - WSishida
Instagram - ishidawrites
Twitter - @ishidaAuthor

Website - www.wsishida.com

~

Printed in Great Britain
by Amazon

71568872R00061